Sisters
A Summer Vacation

HakJin Kim

창조와 지식

Sisters
A Summer Vacation

Hak Jin Kim

Characters

- Bora Kang
- Lang Lee (Bora's half-sister)
- Jung Lee (Wan's older sister, Bora and Lang's older cousin)
- The twins (Lang's brothers, Bora and Jung's cousins)
- HyoSun Lee (grandmother, the senior of the Lee family)
- Maria (housekeeper)

- Jin Kim
- Joon Kim (Jin's father, Hyun's second son)
- Hyun Lee (Jin's grandmother)
- KyungLa Kim (Jin's cousin)

- Brian Bacon (Jin's cousin)
- Joe Bacon (Brian's younger brother)
- Ellen Yoo (Brian's mother, Jin's aunt)

- Kate Thompson (Jin's friend)

- Christine Smith (Jin's friend)

- Henry Miller (Kate and Christine's friend)
- Carl Miller (Henry's older brother)

1

By the time Bora Kang begins to feel bored in the flight from Inchon to LA, she hears an announcement for passengers saying the plane will land at the airport in half an hour. As she puts her seatbelt on, she glances at Lang Lee, her half-sister, who is still asleep next to her. Since Bora flies for the first time in her life, she doesn't let herself drop into a fitful doze all through the flight. After checking Lang's seat belt when a flight crew passes by, she turns her head to see outside from the window seat. The sun blazes down from the blue sky on the Pacific Ocean and the coastline stretched far away. She suddenly realizes that she is flying to California to spend her summer vacation with Lang and their cousins. While staring vacantly at the sky, she thinks of her mother who is left alone for the whole summer working as usual.

As Bora feels sorry about her mother, she looks back on this time last year. Bora, born to an unmarried mother, couldn't think of flying out to LA. She was just a nobody until Lang approached her to be a friend when they were both seniors in high school. Bora was so close to Lang that she could be invited to Lang's home for lunch around the end of that summer. At their lunch table Bora met HyoSun Lee, Lang's grandmother, and the encounter with HyoSun made a big change in Bora's life. During lunch Bora felt HyoSun's eyes on her without knowing what it was all about. Later that year Bora found out why she got attention from HyoSun: Bora looked like her second son who died of a heart attack still young. HyoSun couldn't but suspect that Bora might be her late son's first daughter born to his ex-girlfriend before Lang was born from his marriage. HyoSun didn't speak it out, but she took action to confirm Bora was her granddaughter and her effort paid off. Bora has turned out to be a family member of the Lees as Lang's half-sister and HyoSun's granddaughter. The Lees, a wealthy family with a strong bond, added Bora in the family registry this past spring. Since then Bora has often spent time with Lang and the Lee family although she has still her mother's last name, Kang. Bora always appreciates Lang's and HyoSun's warm supports, without which nothing has happened and her dream to travel to America can't come true.

A slight turbulence on the plane makes Bora stop thinking about the past and glance at Lang who still closes her eyes. As the plane touches down safely, Bora texts to her mother that they landed at the airport.

Bora and Lang feel tired a bit on the long distance flight. They take out their suitcases from an overhead bin and move to the arrivals lounge in silence. Lang looks around and finds Jung Lee, their cousin, in a minute, and Bora is surprised with the dense crowd of people in the lounge.

"Hey, sis!" Lang raises her hand.

Jung comes and looks at Bora.

"Hi, girls, how are you? Aren't you jet-lagged?" Jung says, smiling.

"Not really. You know Bora, don't you?" Lang says.

"Sure! I finally meet you, Bora."

"Hi, sis. I've heard about you a lot. You look great."

"Thanks, Bora. Oh my! You have his eyes. You really look like your late dad, uncle BumKyu. You're really his daughter, huh." Jung smiles at Bora.

While driving to the beach house of the Lee family, Jung talks about the city and local people to Bora, who, in the back seat of the car, listens to Jung and looks out the window. Bora is amazed at the sight of endless traffic on the highway.

They arrive at a big house which Bora saw in the picture hung on the wall of Lang's room in Korea. Bora finds it odd for a moment that she faces the house she longed for. Filled with expectation Bora looks around as she walks in the house, and Lang smiles at Bora.

"Hey, Bora, relax. It's your home. You'll get used to this place."

"Hmm. I feel like I'm dreaming. Lang, I'm happy now. Oh, there's a pool. Fantastic!" Bora is more excited with the pool.

Lang and Bora go upstairs to the room where Bora is supposed to share with Lang until late August. By the time Lang begins her freshman year, she'll leave for a college dorm and Bora goes back to Korea for her second semester of freshman year. After unpacking their bags Bora sits on the window seat while Lang is on the phone. Enraptured with the view of the sea from the bedroom window, Bora thinks of her mother again who has never passed the time away in a beach to relax. As Bora finds that Lang gets off the phone, she looks up at Lang.

"Hey, this view is so beautiful. I think I can sit here all day just watching the waves dashing on the shore," Bora says, smiling.

"Bora, you'll see it for more than a month. Let's go out to the beach"

On their way out through a side door of the backyard, they bump into their twin cousins with their surfboards.

"Oh, you're Bora Kang. Hi, sis, it's very nice to see you. Our grandma told us about you," one of the twins says.

"Hi, how are you guys doing?" Bora says with a big smile.

"We heard you're good at all kinds of sports. Let's go surfing next week."

"Yeah . . . but I've never surfed before," Bora says.

"Don't worry. We'll teach you. You'll do good, sis."

"Absolutely! Boys, we're going out, and see you at dinner." Lang opens the side door.

Lang and Bora walk to the beach where a few sunbathers are lying on their bellies. As soon as Bora gets her feet on the sand, she lets out a gasp of delight at the ocean view.

"Bora, you're just looking at the sea. It's no big deal," Lang says with a smile.

"Yeah, but this view is special to me. I'm on a Californian beach, you know," Bora says, taking a deep breath.

Bora stands still for five minutes or so looking at the horizon. And she points at seals swimming to nearby rocks on the seashore.

"Lang! Look at those seals. Oh, I've never seen seals up close before."

Bora feels happy with the place where she breathes and what she sees at this point. The first day in California looks perfect to Bora with a quiet beach.

2

Bora and Lang get back to their bedroom from the beach and hurry to change their clothes to go out. They will have dinner with the twins and Jung at an upscale restaurant where Jung made a reservation to congratulate Bora on becoming her cousin. Being pleased with a warm welcome, Bora thinks of Wan Lee who can't be together this evening due to his stay in Korea. She feels sorry about it since she shared all the things happening around her with Wan who had once been her close friend and yet became her cousin after she turned into a member of the Lee family. To Bora, he is still the only man she can rely on.

The five young Lees leave for the restaurant in a van driven by Jung, the oldest one. In half an hour they arrive at a fine restaurant and sit at the table. While Bora is looking through the menu, one of the twins asks how Bora has been doing.

"Wait. I need to study the menu. There are so many dishes and each description about it makes me think which one is delicious food for me," Bora says with her eyes fixed on the menu.

"Well, take time!" says Jung.

A few minutes later, a good-looking waitress in uniform asks, "Good evening! Are you ready to order now?"

After ordering food, Bora begins to tell the twins and Jung how Lang and she became close friends.

"Awesome! Sis, if you got out of high school without knowing Lang, we couldn't have any chance to know you. And our grandma played an important role in getting you back. The way of things is mysterious, huh!" says one of the twins.

"By the way, what made you get close to Bora?" the other twin asks Lang.

"Well . . . I've never thought about why I asked Bora to go out for a snack. Perhaps, it was because of beautiful cherry blossoms outside the window or I might have pity on Bora because I saw her being alone without any friend. I don't know . . . Anyway, I wanted to speak to Bora when her profile looked lonely," Lang says, smiling at Bora.

Bora smiles back at Lang.

"Sis Bora, hope to have fun with you as long as you stay here. Oh, I guess we'll see you every summer vacation."

"Yeah, absolutely," the other twin says.

"Do you have any plan, Bora?" Jung asks.

"I don't. But I'll look around the city and the college," Bora says.

"Sis, can we see you do Taekwondo?"

"Yes, tomorrow. By the way, you're speaking Korean, huh. You'd better speak English for me. I think I need to practice it," Bora smiles at the twins.

As they have a great time having chit-chatted with each other, a gorgeous girl passes by and stops in front of Jung.

"Hi, Jung, how are you doing? It's good to see you."

"What a surprise! How have you been, Kate? It's been a long time. How's your school going?" Jung says.

"Guys, this is Kate, a high school junior like you, boys."

"Hi, nice to see you, guys. You're Jung's siblings, right?"

"No, we're cousins."

"Oh, I see. You look like you're having a good time. Great! I've got to go. Have a nice evening! I'll see you around, Jung. Bye," Kate smiles and goes away to her companions.

Looking at Kate's back, Jung explains that she has worked part time as a private math tutor and Kate once was her student when she was a 7th grader.

"She grew up to be a nice girl. I thought she might have a grudge against me 'cause I scolded her several times for her attitude. She mostly didn't listen to me, so . . ." Jung says.

"Really? But she doesn't look like that. Speaking of math, Bora has talent in math. Guys, you can get help with math from Bora," Lang says to the twins.

The twins look at Jung and say, "Yes, we like the sound of that. Jung has no time for us, and we have a lot of math problems to be solved in the SAT prep class." Listening to them, Bora smiles at them and says, "I'm available any time for you."

As there are a lot of conversations going on through the evening, Jung sees her twin cousins laugh with excitement. Bora, giving the strong impression with a healthy physique, seems to play a role as a center for the young generation of the Lee family.

As the night grows dark so that the beach is no longer visible, Bora sits on a twin bed and looks around the room with en-suite bathroom while Lang is taking a shower. It looks cozy with a big window that faces the sea. It is as spacious as Lang's bedroom that Bora saw in Sungbok-dong, but it's simple, with two white bookshelves, twin beds, a small table with two chairs, a window seat and an easy chair by the window. They are all white except two comforters which are golden brown in color. Bora stands up and starts to unpack her luggage. She hangs up her clothes in the white built-in closet and puts some books on the shelf. Unpacking her bag ends soon before Lang finishes showering because she doesn't bring many things. While waiting for her turn to use the bathroom, Bora texts to her mother, "Mom, I returned home with Lang and other cousins. We had a great dinner. Everybody was really nice to me. I feel good. The first day here was exciting. I loved to walk along the beach right in front of the house. And it's Friday night."

3

On the next day, a Saturday, Bora wakes up before the alarm on her mobile phone goes off. She is puzzled a bit for a second when facing a white ceiling from her bed, but she realizes where she is. She tiptoes toward the window seat lest Lang should awake to the sound of her footsteps. Leaning against the wall on the window seat Bora sees the sun rising over the horizon.

At exactly the same time as Bora sees the sun rising, a middle aged man busies himself in making breakfast in a ranch style house a mile from the Lee family's home. The man in his early fifties looks neat with blue Jeans and a yellow striped shirt. The kitchen is clean with all the kitchen utensils nicely kept in their places, and a kitchen island is filled with groceries. Humming with his nose, he washes vegetables and trims fat from beef with his nimble fingers. As he keeps on making noise by turning on the faucet and stirring vegetables in the pot, a bedroom door opens and a teen girl shouts at him.

"Dad, you're too noisy. What time is it?"

"Oh, did I wake you up, Jin?" the man, Joon Kim, says in a high tone.

"Yeah, I don't eat breakfast, and grandma isn't home, you know. Stop doing it, please. I need a rest on Saturday."

"Alright, I'm almost done. So, you can sleep more, sweetie." Joon walks on his tiptoes, trying to be as quiet as he can.

Joon knows that his daughter doesn't eat breakfast on weekends and his mother, Hyun Lee, goes for a jog every Saturday morning so that the food he prepares will go to the freezer. But as long as he has time for cooking, he does it no matter what Jin says.

A while later Joon sits on the sofa with a cup of coffee in his hand and texts his young friend. "What are you gonna do today? I'm planning to go fishing. Will you join me?"

"Call me when you're near my home." Joon gets a text back immediately.

Joon goes to the kitchen to put the food into the fridge to let Jin and Hyun have it conveniently, and then equips himself for a one day fishing trip. When Joon is almost done, Jin comes out of her room.

"Hey, Dad. Are you going fishing? Did you text grandma?" Jin asks.

"Not yet, but I'll do it. And heat up the food before you eat it. See you at night, Jin."

Jin goes to the kitchen after she sees Joon shut the front door behind him. She opens the fridge.

"I wonder why my mouth is watering today. Hmm, let me see . . . oh, there's a sauce for the bread."

Jin sits at the island with a loaf of homemade bread and a sauce for it. She slices the bread and spreads the sauce on it, and bites a piece off. "Oh, this is too good to resist, yummy!" Jin thinks that Joon is not so much a math teacher as a chef.

While Jin enjoys her breakfast, one message pops up. "Hey, Jin, are you awake? What's your plan this afternoon?"

"Hi, Christine, I have to go to my aunt's house. You know, I tutor my cousin as a part-time job."

"Okay, text me when you're done. Kate and I will be waiting

for you at the mall nearby home." Christine texts back to Jin.

Christine and Jin along with Kate have been together since they began their second year in high school. They see almost every day in school and in some fun places on weekends although they live in different neighborhoods. Jin, born to a middle-class Korean family, feels a sense of belonging and highly energized when she walks anywhere, flanked by Christine and Kate who are conspicuous because of their gorgeous looks. Christine and Kate are tall with bodies to die for so that most of school girls want to hang out with them. When Jin entered the high school, she couldn't think of them as her best friends. As an average looking girl, Jin kept them at arm's length because they weren't easy to get along with. Moreover, she had been a loner for a long time without any friends feeling left out at school. Her mother's sudden death caused her to change her ways feeling small in front of others even though her father, Joon, tried to have her make friends by throwing frequent parties and took care of her school stuff. And then things changed when Jin got the credit for math and sports towards the end of her freshman year. She caught the attention of students of her age in school and made friends with Christine and Kate who were cheer leaders about that time.

4

Jin is going to her aunt's house in the hot weather of southern California. Driving her car with the sunroof open, she enjoys a hot breeze blowing against her face. She keeps to the speed limit since she got her driver's license lately. She touches the audio icon and sings along to K-pop songs in a relaxed mood, recalling the time she slept over with KyungLa, her paternal cousin, who now is a college student in Seoul.

Half an hour later Jin sits at the dining table across Brian, her tenth grade cousin, who has given up on math. Brian is only one year younger than Jin, but he doesn't care about being a student in front of Jin. On the contrary, he seems delighted with her tutoring because he hasn't met her for years since his mother, Ellen, didn't want to see Jin. Thanks to his poor grades in school, Ellen welcomed Jin again to their home to let her help him.

    Thinking of Ellen, her maternal aunt, Jin never feels better than when she can see Ellen again. Jin hasn't seen Ellen for years after her mother's death and hasn't even been interested in how Ellen lived her life because she had a grudge against Ellen who had cared for Jin a lot but changed by keeping aloof herself from Jin. Jin who needed Ellen in place of her late mother was upset so much that she didn't want to know about Ellen who had to get through many things. At that time Jin was too young to understand that a big frustration caused by the loss of her only sister made Ellen lose contact with Jin. Recently, Jin had a chance to know that Ellen's husband had cheated on her, so Ellen filed for a divorce before launching her own start-up design studio. As Jin earned some fame for an achievement in math, Ellen visited the Kim family saying sorry for her aloofness and said that she needed Jin as the only person for Brian to help him improve his math and keep up with his schoolwork.

Jin flips the pages of the workbook and asks where they were in the last class. Brian opens his workbook, glancing at Jin.

"This time there was only one question I couldn't handle."

"Really? Let me see it. Oh, good job! Brian."

Jin proceeds to take up new concepts in the next chapter after explaining how to solve the question Brian got wrong. She tries to have him master problem-solving skills and deepen his understanding of basic facts. Looking at Brian, Jin feels proud of him finding that he is making an improvement fast in mathematics.

Brian, born to an American father and a Korean mother, Ellen, is tall with green eyes and curly brown hair. He doesn't talk much nor show an interest in anybody except Jin whom Brian feels comfortable with because Jin is quiet but active like him. Moreover, he becomes excited about K-pop groups and he begins to love to practice Korean language during the class with Jin, who is a fluent Korean speaker. One way and another, Brian can't help enjoying Jin's tutoring.

About two hours later, Jin checks the time on her cell phone and says, "let's call it a day."

"Yep. See you next Saturday, Jin." Brian rises to his feet and goes to his room.

Jin looks around to find her aunt. At that point Ellen

shows up in front of Jin.

"Aunt Ellen, I was about to leave. Brian's doing well."

"Oh, great, thank you. Jin, can I ask a favor?"

"Yes, what is it?"

"Well, I'm wondering if you can babysit Joe for about an hour. Of course, I'll pay you. My close friend called me to come 'cause she got into trouble and needs me now, so . . . "

"Oh, but my friends are waiting for me at the mall. Well . . . okay. But you should come back in an hour, please."

"By the way, do you mind if my friends come over here while waiting for you?" Jin asks.

"No problem. Thank you so much, Jin. I'll be back as soon as possible." Ellen goes out and Jin texts Christine right away.

5

Jin puts her bag on the dining table, hearing a noise from the living room. Joe, Brian's younger brother, sitting in front of TV is cheering for his favorite baseball team.

"Hi, Joe."

"Hi, Jin. Look, there's a Korean pitcher. I love to see him playing."

"Yeah, he's doing great. Hey, will you play basketball?"

"Yes, I'll be with you in a minute. The game's almost over. Oh, yes! He made it! Let's go outside, Jin."

When Joe gets in the garage to get a basketball, Jin texts Brian to ask if he'd like to join them, but she doesn't expect any answer.

Jin and Joe pass the ball to each other around the basketball stand. As Jin scores goals whenever she shoots the ball, Joe looks surprised and becomes more excited. Joe, a seventh grader, has been friendly with everyone unlike Brian so that he has been often invited to a sleepover. His outgoing character made Ellen's life easier as a single mother. Things always happened with Brian who didn't talk with Ellen although she could handle things whatever it takes.

Jin texts Brian again to let him come out and play together and then sees Christine's car pulling into the driveway.

"Hey, Jin. You're playing basketball," says Kate, opening the passenger door.

Joe turns his head and rolls his eyes. "Wow!"

"You have an eye for pretty things, kid," Christine says.

"Yeah, I have." Joe giggles.

"Girls, do you wanna join us?" Jin asks.

"No, let's get inside. I brought snacks," Kate says.

When Jin opens the front door, she bumps into Brian.

"Brian! Oh, gosh, you scared me. I thought you were in your room," Jin says with her eyes wide open.

"I just heard the noise outside the window," Brian says, shrugging his shoulders.

"Hmm, let me introduce my friends. Christine and Kate."

"Hi, Brian," Kate says with a smile.

"Hi, Kate," Brian glances at Christine.

"Guys, shall we eat doughnuts? Brian, can we have some milk, please?" Christine says.

Sweet doughnuts as an afternoon snack make all of them feel comfortable and lighten the mood. Although two girls except Jin are strangers to Brian and Joe, they have a nice chat together. Jin can see that Brian, an introvert, looks excited with her friends.

"Guys, let's bring up an idea about what we have to do now," Jin says.

"Would you like to go inline skating?" Joe suggests.

"That's a good idea. I know there is an inline skating rink inside the nearby park. We can rent skates. Do you wanna go?" Jin says.

"I'm in." Brian raises his right index finger.

"But I can't skate. I can watch you skating," Kate says, glancing at Christine.

"I'll help you do it."

"Okay. But you should help me not fall on my back." Kate agrees to go skating.

Jin texts Ellen to have permission for their outing.

Around 4 o'clock Christine pulls her car into the parking lot with surprise because it is full. After roaming for a few minutes she can manage to find room for her car and parks it. When Christine and Kate get off the car, they see Jin coming along with Brian and Joe.

"Jin, I think the rink is crowded, huh."

"Yeah, hmm . . . Surprise! Look who's here! Isn't that Henry Miller?" Jin says, pointing to a man.

"Yeah, I can't believe it. I'm wondering if he comes with a girl," Kate says.

At that moment, Henry turns his head to the girls and comes to them.

"Hey, I didn't expect you here. Oh, this is my brother, Carl, a freshman at USC."

"Hello, I'm Carl."

"Carl wanted to go surfing, but we're here," Henry says, looking at Kate.

"Guys, let's go inside," Kate says, clapping her hands.

Rental booth is lined up with people, and Brian whispers to Jin that he'd like to go home. Jin insists that he stay with her because she has companions. Then Henry interrupts their conversation.

"Guys, can we go to VR Zone? It's fun."

"Yes! I can. Who else? This place is so crowded," Joe says, making a fuss.

The rest of them agree with Henry on his suggestion.

They go off to their respective cars and drive to a huge shopping mall near the beach.

6

About that time when Jin and her companions are on their way to a VR game room, Bora and Lang are wandering around the mall after having late lunch at the food court. They have planned to watch a movie but changed to spend time at a big bookstore. After a couple of hours in the bookstore, they begin to walk down the hallway.

"This place is huge." Bora snoops around.

"Oh, look, there is VR Zone across the way."

They stop at VR Zone, a game room in which visitors experience virtual reality playing VR games and explore their virtual world after wearing some special gear. Bora says to Lang that she had been to this place in Seoul and enjoyed virtual world with expensive tickets. They see that there are more than twenty stations which have various kinds of VR equipment and young people stand in a long line at each station.

"Wow, look at those people," Lang says.

"Yeah, but it's worth the wait," Bora says, glancing at Lang.

"Do you wanna do it? I'll buy tickets."

"I'll pay mine, Lang."

"No, Bora. Everything is on me. Our grandma gave me her credit card," Lang says.

After getting tickets for ten stations, Bora and Lang get in line. They stick together whenever they go to each station lest Bora should get lost though it can't happen this time. They are having fun, being thrilled with each VR device. When they are going out of the game room after using up their tickets, Bora sees a group of teenagers near the ticket desk and finds that a girl approaches Bora.

"Hi, I saw you last night. You were having dinner with Jung. I'm Kate."

"Oh, yes, you're Kate. It's nice to see you again. Lang, do you remember her?" Bora says, looking at Lang.

"Yeah. I'm Lang. This is Bora. How nice we meet you here!" Lang says.

"Are you leaving? We've just arrived. We should've been here earlier. Well . . . it's not a good idea if I let you go like this. Can I have your phone number?" Kate asks.

Lang gives her US phone number and Bora give hers which is allocated by a USIM chip equipped inside her phone.

"My number is available until early August," Bora says with a smile.

"I'll call you next week," Kate says and goes to her friends.

Lang and Bora look at each other for a second and sit on a nearby bench.

"Kate thinks we're high school students like her. Should we tell her we're college girls? Oh, well, it doesn't make any difference though," Lang says, shrugging her shoulders.

"Yeah, but I'm interested in Kate and her friends. So, I wanna hang out with them. How about you, Lang?"

"As you wish."

"Oh, Jung is at the parking lot now. Let's go, Bora," Lang says.

On the way home, Jung says that Lang will have her own car a couple of days later.

"Before then, I'll give you a ride."

In the beach house, the housekeeper, Maria, who has worked for years is still in the kitchen doing house chores. As soon as she sees Bora, she introduces herself and asks what kind of food Bora would like to have. Bora smiles at her and says, "I'd love to eat whatever you cook. Thanks."

At the dinner table Bora begins to talk about how excited she was in the VR Zone and the twins agree with her since they visit there once a week. Bora, having a strong square jaw and thick eyebrows, raises the mood by her bright smile. While looking at Bora talking a lot, Lang thinks of the past when she met Bora who had been quiet all the time in school and feels a sense of pride for having changed Bora to be such an energetic and active person.

7

Under the hot sun, Lang is lying on her belly browsing her cell phone, and Bora is reading a thriller lying on her back on a big towel with a wide-brimmed hat on. They get tanned enough to look like girls from the Caribbean since they go to the beach nearly every day. Their faces are wet with sweat, but it doesn't seem like they get out of the sun.

"Bora, we're gonna stay here until noon. Oh, I forgot to tell you this. Brother Wan doesn't come to us this summer."

"Really? He didn't even text me, huh."

"I guess that he didn't wanna let you down by texting directly to you."

"I'm sorry to hear that, hmm. Well, what's your plan for this afternoon?" Bora asks, shrugging her shoulders.

"How about going to see a movie?"

"Sounds good to me."

In a second Bora's cell phone vibrates.

"Hello?" Bora answers with a quivering voice due to her poor English.

"Hi, this is Kate. Surprise, huh? How're you doing? Do you have time tomorrow evening?" Kate says.

"Uh⋯, yes. Why are you asking?"

"I wanna invite you to my home. I'll throw a pizza party. My parents are supposed to go to a social function and will be home late, and they allowed me to do that. Oh, my older brother is out of town. So, will you join us?" Kate asks.

"Me and Lang?"

"Yes! Come around six o'clock. I'll text you my address. See you tomorrow." Kate gets off the phone.

"Lang, Kate invited us to her home tomorrow. Don't say no." Bora seems excited.

"Yeah, I told you. I'll go with you wherever you want to go. By the way I heard she invited you only, and she included me when you asked . . . " Lang says.

"Are you upset? Come on. You know, she called in order of alphabet." Bora tries to please Lang.

"Okay. Bora, I'll drive my car tomorrow."

"Hey, don't make a face, Bora! I practiced driving a lot of time," Lang smiles a bit.

"Yep, I believe you."

"Lang, are you done with registration for the classes?" Bora asks.

"Not yet. I made an appointment with an advisor to talk about my degree requirement. You know, I already planned my course schedule, and I know my registration access date."

"Can I go with you when you see your advisor? I'd like to look around the campus."

"Sure, I told you. We go together everywhere." Lang smiles at Bora.

In the afternoon of the next day Bora makes cupcakes to bring to the party with the help of the housekeeper because she is new to the kitchen of the beach house.

With two boxes of cupcakes, Lang and Bora arrive at Kate's home, a big fenced house. As Lang parks her car on the street in front of the house, she watches an Asian girl with a tall boy walking across the street. Lang turns her head to Bora and asks if they should hang out with those high school students.

"Should we have turned down Kate's invitation?" Lang asks.

"Well, Jung knows who Kate is. So, I think there'll be no problem at all." Sensing Lang's hesitation, Bora tries to allay her worry.

Bora walks ahead of Lang a few minutes after the Asian girl goes inside Kate's house. When Bora and Lang stand at the house, the front door is flung open before Bora's finger touches the doorbell.

"Hi, welcome to my home." Kate gives a big smile to Lang and Bora.

"Here! These are homemade cupcakes," says Bora, showing boxes.

"Wow, thanks. You shouldn't have!" Kate makes a cute smile.

Bora and Lang hear a noise that seems to come from a room with a high ceiling.

"Hey, here are newcomers."

As soon as Kate speaks out loud, everybody in the room casts glances at Bora and Lang, and an Asian girl comes near to Lang.

"My name is Jin Kim. I'm Korean American. I think I've

heard about you a little. We welcome you both to our evening."

"Hi, thanks. I'm Lang and this is Bora. Bora is a college freshman at SNU in Seoul and this fall I'll be a college student."

"Wow, you're college girls. I think we'll need your advice some day. Oh, let me tell you this. We don't do drugs. By the way, my cousin is a student at SNU. What a small world! Do you know KyungLa?"

"No, I don't. But when I go back to Seoul next month, I can get in touch if you give me her cell phone number," Bora says.

"You see, I'm a good judge of a character," says Kate, giving a big smile at Jin.

At that point pizzas arrive.

8

"Guys, table is ready. Come over here!" Kate says loudly.

On the big dining table different kinds of pizza are arranged.

"Guys, I hope you won't mind eating together. I just wanna to have time to get to know each other."

Kate seems to be busy as a host setting the table with beverages and plates.

"Bora, Lang, I think you want beer."

"Hey, I need beer, too," Carl raises his hand.

"Okay! Now, everything is all set. Before starting, I wanna say this. I'm very happy to have you all here. And I wanna thank Lang and Bora for accepting my invitation. Lang and Bora just came to LA a few days ago. How do I know it? I saw them at the restaurant when I said hello to Jung who was my tutor. Oddly enough, I felt familiar with Bora and Lang at first sight. Thankfully, we happened to bump into at VR Zone. And, here are Bora and Lang." Kate looks at Bora and Lang by turns to let them stand up.

Bora rises to her feet first.

"Hello, my name is Bora. It's not easy to speak English, but I can say I'm very happy here with you. I'm a college freshman in Seoul. I'm going to study in engineering. Thanks."

Lang begins to talk about herself soon after. Carl seems to pay attention to Lang, especially when she says that she's going to USC.

"Oh, you're a USC student. We'll see at the campus then. I'm Carl. I think we have a lot of things to share."

As soon as Lang sits, Jin takes a piece of pepperoni pizza saying that she already told Bora and Lang about herself and let Christine take her turn. As people introduce themselves, Bora and Lang learn that Jin speaks Korean fluently and her good looking cousin, Brian, loves to meet Korean people. Kate and Christine have been close friends long before Jin joined them as a friend. Henry, who is Carl's younger brother, and other three girls go to the same high school and Brian, Jin's cousin, is in the tenth grade going to a private high school.

Brian stares at Bora with curious attention and Bora doesn't avoid his gaze thinking that he has beautiful green eyes.

"Bora, let's go to the living room. I'd like to talk about your college and some stuff you've done in Korea," Brian says, coming near to Bora.

Bora stands up sipping her can of beer and follow Brian to the couch in front of a huge TV. Soon the dining room is empty as Carl leaves his seat with haste to go after Lang who is chasing Bora.

In the living room, there is BTS's music in the air. Kate begins to dance to the rhythm of the music and Henry dances with his shoulders.

"Wow, BTS is really popular all over the world. Do you like K-pop?" Bora asks Brian.

"Well, so so. I don't like to listen to the music. It's noisy. But I like to know about Korean people 'cause my mom is Korean American. I've never been to Korea. I just watched it through YouTube."

While Brian goes on talking, Jin sits next to Bora grabbing with a bite of cupcake and interrupts Brian after winking at him.

"Oh, Bora, the cupcake tastes so good. How did you make it?

Can I have a recipe for my dad? My dad is good at cooking."

"Really? I'll send you a text message with the recipe. What's your phone number?"

Jin and Bora exchange their cell phone numbers right away and Brian gets Bora's one.

"Bora, I really wanna visit Korea next summer. Will you spare your time for me then?"

"Sure, I'd love to do. It'll be exciting if I show you Seoul and my college campus."

"Thanks in advance."

While talking with Brian and Jin, Bora keeps checking up on Lang to see if she drinks beer. Lang looks like she is enjoying being with Carl who becomes her college friend. Bora looks out the French door which leads to the backyard garden and a swimming pool. The sun has already set, but the dim light of dusk is enough for you to see what's going on outside. Bora texts Lang that they'd better go home before it's too late, and she sees Lang going out to the backyard with Carl.

9

As it gets dark by the minute, Bora begins to feel nervous and turns a deaf ear to Brian and Jin. She texts Lang again, "Lang, we should go. It's almost nine. Answer me, please." There's no answer from Lang. Bora cuts in when Jin is speaking.

"Jin, I'm sorry to cut you off. I think something has happened to Lang. I texted Lang several times, but there is no answer. I saw that she went out to the backyard about thirty minutes ago. I'm worrying about her so much."

"Bora, you don't have to worry. She's with Carl. What makes you so nervous? They may stroll around the pool." Jin looks outside and rises to her feet.

"We'd better go out to the pool," says Jin.

Brian follows Jin with Bora. They shut the French door behind them and walk toward the pool to look for Lang and

Carl, but there is no one in the dim light of lamps glowing in the backyard garden. All of sudden, they wonder how come Lang and Carl got out of the house without noticing and even texting anyone. Bora knows instinctively that something is wrong because Lang isn't that person who slips out of the house without Bora.

"You see? Something's wrong. Let Henry call his brother."

They get inside and shout to Henry.

"Henry, make a phone call to Carl right now. Carl and Lang disappeared."

"What? Let me check the kitchen door. I locked it before you guys came," Kate says.

Kate gets back to the living room.

"It's locked, huh. Then they should get in through the French door. Did they leap over the fence? I don't understand what's going on. Bora, did you call Lang on the phone?"

"Yes, I keep calling her, but . . . oh my god. Why is this happening? I should've been with her. I had kept watching her until she went outside with Carl." Bora is on the verge of derangement.

"Bora, I'll call the police after checking on two places, my room and Carl's car," Kate says.

At that moment, the bell rings. Kate looks at Bora and the others in the room stare at the front door.

"Isn't that Carl?" Kate mumbles.

"Wait, Kate. Don't open it. What if strangers stand at the door?"

"Come on, Bora. You watched too many thriller movies," Christine says.

"Not movies, books. Kate, why don't you peep through a wide-angle lens," Bora says.

Kate peeps through the lens and opens the door.

"Oh my! You're here. Where have you been? We were freaked out. We were gonna call the police."

"We're so sorry for all the trouble. You know what? We were abducted, but we're here, guys. It's really strange how we reached a place about a half mile from here. Luckily, I found out where we were, so we walked all the way down here. I don't remember how we got there. I just remember we were at a fence door and I think we passed out when we opened it."

"Do you have a CCTV, a surveillance camera outside the house?" Bora asks grabbing Lang who looks weary.

"Yes. Guys, let's go to the kitchen and let's watch the CCTV footage. And let me tell you this, Bora, the French door is locked now." Kate smiles at Bora who seems like a meticulous girl.

In the kitchen, Kate plays the footage and the other seven people focus on the screen wondering what happened in the backyard. Strangely enough, no one joined Carl and Lang who were talking and going toward a narrow fence door attached to the house and gone. At that scene, Kate points to the fence door and shrugs her shoulders.

"Oh, there has been a door, huh. I didn't know that. Hey, Carl, you went out for yourself with Lang. We don't get it."

"Believe us. We can't remember where we headed after we reached the fence door. We remember someone whispered from outside the fence, so we walked to the fence door and opened it. That's all I can remember. We must have blacked out," Lang says in a small voice.

"Do you have another footage taken from the front entrance of the house?" Henry asks.

"We'll see. Oh, what the heck, the camera didn't work. We can't see who showed up here. Someone might take Carl and Lang by car, but we can't find anything about the car and strangers." Kate looks perplexed.

"By the way, are you okay? You didn't get hurt, did you?" Christine asks Carl and Lang.

"We're fine. But Carl said his cell phone was stolen. I didn't have mine with me at that point. It was in my purse," Lang says.

Bora breathes a sigh of relief.

"Do we have to report to the police?" Brian asks.

"Not now. I'd better tell my parents first. But, Carl, you have to report your cell phone missing," says Kate. "Well . . . I think you guys can go home if you want to."

"Kate, we won't leave you alone in this situation," Jin says.

"Bora, Lang, I think you'd better go home now. And I'm so sorry for this weird situation. This is the first time we've had this happening since I've lived in this neighborhood for almost ten years."

"Don't mention it. It wasn't your fault. It just happened. And I came back without any harm. I thank you for everything. We enjoyed pizza and the chit-chat." Lang smiles at Kate and the other people.

"I'm so sorry, Lang. It's very kind of you to say so." Kate stares at Lang and bites her lip.

Bora also says that she was so scared when Lang disappeared but she feels fine because Lang is back safely.

Bora and Lang hear the door shut behind them as they go to Lang's car. While walking, Bora checks around to see anyone hanging around and gets ready for any attack. Nothing happens, and Lang starts the engine saying, "I'm safe with you. It was a long night."

10

While driving home from Kate's house, Lang doesn't talk, keeping her eyes on the road. Sitting on the passenger seat, Bora is tense worrying about Lang who got through an odd experience. About 20 minutes later Lang's car enters the luxury residential neighborhood, and Bora feels a whoosh of air.

"Lang, did you feel it like I did?" Bora asks.

"What do you mean, Bora?"

Lang begins to check the tires as soon as she gets off the car.

"Oh my gosh! I got a flat tire. You know, this is a brand new car," Lang says with a surprise.

"Lang, what if they did this?"

"They?" Lang asks.

A Summer Vacation • 49

"I mean the people who took you and Carl tonight. Anyway, it's my fault. I shouldn't have accepted the invitation. I'm so sorry, Lang." Bora is close to tears.

"Bora, don't be sorry. I enjoyed the party while talking with Carl. And you should hang out with Americans since you're in LA. Am I right?" Lang smiles at Bora.

As Bora and Lang finish taking a shower, Lang brings some beer.

"Let's relax. I couldn't drink more than a sip at Kate's house. Would you like a drink, Bora?"

"Sure. Thanks."

Bora sits on her twin bed stretching her legs and Lang sits in an easy chair by the window. They just drink beers in silence for a while, and Bora looks at Lang with curious eyes. Lang's eyes meet Bora's and Lang says, "I can see you wanna know what I did with Carl. You know, he's a funny guy. He has a good heart. I think we have a lot in common. But I still don't understand how I can't remember anything about that happening."

"Hmm . . . Bora, let's forget the bad thing about tonight. Let's not talk to our grandma about this happening."

"Okay, I'll try."

As night goes on, Bora keeps coming up with Lang's awful experience two hours ago while looking at Lang who falls into a sleep as soon as she drinks up a can of beer. It shows how much of a hard time she had had until she got home. No matter how hard Bora thinks about it, it is inconceivable that Carl and Lang could have been taken by someone in the middle of the party. On the basis of several circumstances, it feels like that the abduction was meticulously planned beforehand. From the surveillance camera that wasn't working at that point, Bora is convinced that there was a deliberate action done by those who intended to take Lang away and the camera was covered with a piece of cloth by them. She also comes to think that Kate may get involved in this scheme due to her dubious attitude like her unawareness of a fence door. At this point, Bora tries to infer who they were and why they did it, but to find suspects is beyond her ability. The more she thinks, the more things become complicated. Bora sighs and mumbles, "why on earth did they take Lang and Carl and release them in a short time? Is it to rob Carl and Lang of their cell phones? Well, I really have no idea who they are. Oh, it's too late to clear up my thoughts." She tries to sleep after being tucked up in bed.

Next morning Bora wakes up early with frightening feeling caused by a weird dream. In her dream Bora was chased by Carl and Kate whose eyes were gleaming with amusement. They were giggling at Bora. Kate was holding a rope in her hand and Carl had a baseball bat. Falling into a deadly fear, Bora ran as fast as she could to get away. But they got closer to Bora and Carl stretched out his hand to grab Bora. At that moment, Bora opened her eyes.

Bora feels odd about her dream wondering why they appeared in her dream even with tools such as a baseball bat and some rope. Since Bora can't go back to sleep, she sits on the window seat and looks outside with her elbow on the windowsill. The sun is already high diffusing light over the ocean though it's about six o'clock. Bora wants to talk to Lang about her dream, but she stays put in silence because Lang is in deep sleep. Bora tries to understand what her dream means and adapt it to the situation Lang has been in. She knows it's absurd to apply her nightmare dream to match reality, but it feels like her dream tells her what happened at

Kate's home.

Lang sleeps through the alarm, and Bora stands up to turn off the alarm for her. A few minutes later, Lang wakes up in the end. Lang looks around the room trying to keep her eyes open as if she is in a strange place.

"Good morning, Lang. How was your sleep?"

"I slept really deep. Did you sleep well too?"

"Well, I woke up early and had a nightmare, you know."

"Really? What was it about?"

Bora tells Lang about what she saw and who chased her with dangerous tools. While listening to Bora, Lang can't hide her fear with her narrow eyes wide open.

"It sounds horrible, but to say the truth, I don't buy it. I mean it's just a nightmare. I think it's just a silly dream." Lang doesn't take it seriously.

"Bora, stop talking about your dream and let's go to the beach after breakfast."

11

Bora can't dispel her nightmare, raising suspicions about Kate and Carl. Bora doesn't have any information about Carl, but she feels like she can't think of him as a trustworthy person. The fact that Carl and Lang go to the same college makes Bora worry about Lang more than ever because Lang seems to like to hang out with Carl to fit into the college. Lang grew up in a sheltered environment with a soft heart, whereas Bora has taken care of herself living with her single working mother. She feels obliged to protect Lang since Bora turned out to be Lang's half sister six months ago. Bora can't let Lang be in trouble whatever it takes, especially when Bora can't be around Lang in LA.

About a week after the party at Kate's house, Bora gets a

phone call from HyoSun, and hears that HyoSun can't come to LA due to her health. Although she is feeling disappointed because she has expected to stay with her grandmother under the same roof for the first time ever, Bora tries to please HyoSun by telling how happy she is in the beach house along with Lang and her cousins. Bora describes about how she saw the city and things around her, keeping her mouth shut about the incident at Kate's house. She also doesn't forget saying how grateful she is to HyoSun for becoming her grandmother. After talking with HyoSun, Bora looks around the house to find Lang, but she can see only Maria in the kitchen. Since Bora knows that Jung is busy at work and twin cousins are taking summer prep classes, Bora has become focused on Lang who makes Bora feel to be her guardian.

Bora texts Lang. Surprisingly, Bora finds out that Lang goes out to meet Carl.

"How could you go out without me?"

"Sorry, Bora, Carl asked for a ride by texting. So I'm on my way."

"Hey, come back. Speaking of it, he has his brother, Henry, or his mother."

Lang doesn't text back any more. All of sudden, Bora has goose bump from imagining something bad would happen to Lang. In a second Bora looks up Jin's cell phone number.

"Hello, this is Bora. Can I talk to you for a minute? Lang is driving to Carl because he asked her for a ride. But I don't get it. He met her only once."

"Hey, Bora. Calm down. Why are you so nervous? He's Henry's brother. There is no problem, I guess."

"Really? Well, do me a favor. Can you ask Carl where he's waiting for Lang?"

"Sure, I'll ask Kate for you 'cause I don't have his number."

A few minutes later Bora gets the answer from Jin.

"I called Christine 'cause Kate didn't answer and found out that Carl went surfing and he didn't call anyone," Jin says.

"Bora, are you sure Lang went to pick up Carl?"

"Yes, Lang texted me she was on the way to Carl."

"That doesn't make sense. Anyway, you just keep calling Lang and I'll talk to Christine and Kate."

"Okay, thanks, Jin."

Bora goes to the kitchen to take a glass of water. She can't calm down, having no idea what to do right now. Bora doesn't know where Lang is heading and can't help but wait for Lang's text. Sitting at the kitchen table, Bora begins to call Lang on her cell phone, but can't reach her. Almost fifteen minutes have passed, and Bora gets a call from Jin.

"It's me, Jin. Did you talk with Lang? Kate doesn't answer her phone right now. Do you know where Lang was driving?"

"No, Lang didn't text about it. What if there is something terribly wrong with her . . . I'm scared to death."

"Hey, Bora, don't be afraid. Lang knows about the city. She'll call you back when she gets to the place where she headed to."

"It's been almost thirty minutes since I got her message."

At that moment an incoming call pops up on Bora's phone screen. It's a call from Kate.

"Oh, I got a call from Kate. Jin, I'll talk to you later."

"Hello, Kate? What's up?"

"Hi, Bora, I'm with Lang. I bumped into her in the mall. Lang's cell phone battery died, so I'm calling you."

"Can you put Lang on?"

"Sure, . . . wait . . . she was right here next to me, but I can't see her right now. Oh, there she is. Lang! Bora wanna talk to you."

Bora waits breathlessly for Lang. At last she hears Lang speak over the phone.

"Lang, you scared me! Why didn't you call me back? Didn't you see numerous phone calls from me?"

"I'm so sorry, Bora. I should've texted you before you went crazy. I just got in this place and found my phone battery was dead. And then, I bumped into Kate."

"Did you meet Carl?" Bora asks as if she doesn't know where Carl is now.

"No, I called Carl on the number from which the text was, but it wasn't his cell phone. So I really felt weird for a minute, and I was about to call you but the battery was gone. And then I bumped into Kate. I was so pleased I could call you on her cell."

While listening to Lang, Bora thinks that Lang is so sloppy as to dash out the door without checking the phone battery.

"Oh, Lang, it's so like you. Which mall are you now?"

"You know, the one where we often hanged out. Bora, I brought my charger. Don't worry. I'll go home as soon as I charge my phone."

"Alright, just call me when you leave the mall, please,"

Bora says.

Lang turns around to give Kate her phone back. At that point Lang notices that Kate looks around as if she is expecting to meet someone, and Lang tries to see who are loitering about the hall. Lang taps Kate on the shoulder and says, "Thanks. Kate, it was a pleasure to see you. What brings you here? Are you supposed to meet Jin and Christine? I know three of you are close."

Kate smiles at Lang without answering and says that she'll have some coffee while Lang charges up her phone battery. They sit at a table in a cafe which is located in the aisle to the exit. Lang is taking a sip of coffee while Kate is on her cell phone texting to someone. Lang glances at Kate wondering why she is with Kate who doesn't like to speak to her, and just then she sees people taking stairs down toward the exit in a tremendous hurry. They are shouting, "Run! Run! We heard gunshots upstairs!"

"What? Oh my god! Let's get out of here!" Lang and Kate shout at the same time.

Instantly, they run toward the exit with their stuff and get to their respective cars.

12

When Kate gets in her car, only then does she see a bunch of police cars with sirens blaring stop in a row near the exits of the mall. Some police officers force a passage through a crowd who makes a rush for the exits while others scan the crowd in search of a gunman. Looking at a chaotic scene in the rearview mirror, Kate starts the engine and drives slowly with one hand on the steering wheel and holds her cell phone with the other to call someone.

"Hey, Henry, it's me. You didn't show up, huh. What makes you think you can stand me up?"

"Oh, I'm sorry. I should've been there, but I couldn't. Carl wanted to go surfing, so I'm down in the beach. By the way why should I go to see you and Lang. She's not my type."

"Yeah? Anyway, I'm leaving the mall 'cause there were

gunshots inside the mall. Oh, crazy people! See you around."

After getting off the phone, Kate feels pathetic about herself. In fact, it was Kate who texted Lang on her brother's phone by Carl's name asking for a ride this afternoon. Kate knows it shouldn't be like the way it is, but she can't control her mind since she encountered Jung at a restaurant about two weeks ago. Kate hasn't thought of Jung for years who had often nagged at her as her math tutor after she got C in math. But all things with Jung in the past brought on the latent hatred toward Jung when Kate happened to see Jung. She has kept dredging up memories with Jung and imagined her childish revenge on Jung. And then she came up with an idea about playing tricks on her cousin because Jung is now out of her reach as a career woman at a big company. As the one whom Kate wanted screw over, Kate chose Lang who looks like a docile girl instead of Bora, a tall stout girl. Strangely, Kate saw Bora as an amazing person who may affect her in some way.

A short time later, the police cars with lights flashing run past her car. It brings Kate back to the moment she got out of the mall where there was a gunshot incident.

"Oh, boy, it feels like I'm doing wrong and I have to stop what's on my mind," Kate mumbles.

"I need Jin's advice. She may find a solution to my problem."

Kate texts Jin, "Call me when you have time. I'm free anytime today."

In the evening, Kate gets a call back from Jin who has just finished her shift at a fast food restaurant where she works as a part-time job.

"Hey, what's up? Do you wanna see me now?" Jin says.

"Yes. Will you come to my home?"

"Is Christine coming?" Jin asks.

"No, I just wanna have a talk with you. It's not a secret, though," Kate says.

"I got it! I'll be there in thirty minutes."

Jin feels a bit uncomfortable because Kate wants to see her without Christine. Kate has been much closer to Christine than Jin, but unusually for Kate, Christine is excluded. While driving, Jin thinks of what she heard from Bora. When Jin was on the phone with Bora, whatever the reason was, she felt that Bora was nervous about Kate and Carl. Bora told Jin that she was suspicious of Carl who called Lang for a ride, and Bora added how Kate could show up by chance at that moment. So, Jin tried to soothe Bora's nerves explaining that there must be an unusual coincidence, but she felt odd about that. As long as Lang is a college girl, she can't misread whoever texted her.

Jin pulls her car along the street in front of Kate's home. She calls her grandmother to say that she'll be home an hour later due to meeting Kate.

There are only two of them in Kate's home, but Kate takes Jin to her room with drink in hand.

"Jin, I just wanna talk with you without Christine 'cause she's simple and doesn't like to think anything seriously. Well . . . I don't know what to say . . . You know, I think my mind is having trouble thinking of someone." Kate starts to talk with a twisted smile.

"You don't know who Jung is. She's Bora and Lang's older cousin and was my math tutor. I've never interested in Jung, but the encounter with her two weeks ago drove me to do a bad thing. Speaking of her, she gave me a sense of humiliation. She wouldn't think like that, but to me she was awful at that time."

"Really? What made you think so? Well . . . she must have made a mistake. I mean she couldn't realize what she did. She might want you to do well on your math . . . but she should be considerate toward you. Kate, I want you to let it go. You have a lot of things to do. And your parents are rich, so why should you pay attention to Jung and her cousins," Jin says.

"You know what? Their family owns a big company. They have nothing to envy anyone like me. Hmm, so I hate to see them happy."

"Come on, Kate, don't be silly! You have a lot! You're gorgeous and smart. You have a fabulous car, and you don't have to work for your college tuition fee. There are so many things I feel envy at. Forget the feeling of humiliation. I hope you thank for everything, especially, you have mom."

"Oh, Jin, I'm sorry for the loss of your mother. I haven't thought about that." Kate looks at Jin warmly.

"You're absolutely right, Jin. I went wrong. After hearing you talk, I know I was so self-centered. Thank you so much for your help. You're cool!"

Kate smiles at Jin, but knows that she won't let it go easily.

"Kate, the other day . . . I mean the day you threw the pizza party. I wonder if your parents found out who took Carl and Lang?"

"Not yet. They reported it to the police, I guess. They were back safely, so the police didn't seem to care about it. So, it was out of my mind."

"Oh, I see. Kate, I say one more time. Just let it go and keep your things in mind such as SAT. We don't have much time for that."

"Yeah, you're absolutely right. Oh, thanks, Jin! You're really my friend. Shall we have supper together?"

"I'd love to, but Joon, my dad, will get ready for dinner for me and my grandma."

"Okay, then, I'll let you go, Jin. Bye now." Kate puts her hand on Jin's shoulder.

Jin gets in her car and texts Bora that there is nothing wrong with Kate. Meanwhile, Bora thinks that Jin is a fair-minded girl who regards her friends as angels.

13

Bora has about two weeks left to fly back to Korea. For three weeks while staying in LA, Bora has had an iffy feeling about something that she can't clearly express. Although she had the pleasure of reading books lying in the sand on the beach with Lang every morning, overall, Bora doesn't feel content, missing her mother and the sound of Sungbok Stream near her home in Korea. Besides, when thinking of Kate, Bora feels even shame at herself regretting her trust in Kate. Bora still thinks that she made haste to open her mind to Kate with a desire to have an American friend. And in consequence, an awful incident happened to Lang at Kate's house, which makes Bora feel like doing something for Lang who seems vulnerable to anyone. As her six month older half sister, Bora feels responsible for whatever happens to Lang.

One afternoon, when Lang has an appointment with an advisor at college, Bora gets a phone call from Kate. Bora ignores the call and follows Lang to the car. Soon after, Bora sees several messages popped up on her cell phone while she is in the hallway of the college building where Lang has a meeting with her advisor. She ignores them again thinking that Kate cannot be trusted and also capricious enough to do some unexpected things. Even though her mind wanders as to Kate's messages, Bora sits on a bench and she takes out a book from her backpack to read. Bora, a bookworm, gets quickly absorbed in what she's reading, and she doesn't notice who are standing next to her.

"Hi, Bora, are you waiting for Lang?"

Bora raises her eyes to see who is talking to her. She is startled to see Kate and Carl and stammers for a second.

"Oh, what brings you here? What a surprise to see you here."

"Yeah? You didn't answer me, so I texted Lang. Did you do it on purpose? It feels like you do." Kate says looking at Bora in the eyes.

Bora takes eyes off Kate and tries to keep reading and says, "you got me wrong. I just didn't know you called me.

That's it. And you can't be my friend 'cause I'm three years older than you."

"Oh, I see. You know what? I just bumped into Carl, a college guy here, right in front of this building. I'm saying this in case you're wondering why I'm here with him,"

"Hi, Carl. How have you been? By the way, Kate, do you have business with me?"

"Yes, I'm just wondering if you can tutor me in math. I know it sounds like a ridiculous request."

"No, I don't think so. I'm sorry. I'll stay here for less than three weeks," Bora says, wondering how Kate knew she is good at math.

"Then, only two weeks will be fine with me." Kate smiles at Bora.

Bora feels perplexed, but she smiles back at Kate saying that it isn't easy to improve her math grade for only two weeks.

"Kate, you have Jin and Christine to study together for math. Oh, there she is! Lang, are you done?" Bora rises to her feet.

"Oh, it's good to see you both. I didn't expect you to be here," Lang says.

"Hi, Lang, welcome to USC. I'll give you a tour of the

college campus."

"Thanks."

Carl takes three girls to a cafeteria for some drink after showing them around. They sit around a table sipping coffee. Kate looks sullen, and Bora doesn't care about her. After casting glances at Kate, Bora speaks to her.

"Hey, Kate, I can teach you taekwondo instead of math if you're interested in it. I'll show you how you can protect yourself."

And then, Bora says to herself, "Don't even think about walking all over Lang and me." Bora knows that there is no ground to consider Kate as a wrongdoer, but she can't help but think of Kate as a twisted girl.

Right after Bora's suggestion, Carl says that he can provide his home for taekwondo demonstration and Kate agrees with him smiling at him. Bora also accepts Carl's offer as she takes a closer look at him across the table at this time. She thinks that there is nothing wrong with Carl in terms of his character.

The next day Bora and Lang get a message from Carl, "I'd like to change the place and the date. I think a small park near my house is better than my home. It's gonna be a picnic. Please write back to me if you aren't okay with it." Lang texts back to Carl that a park is convenient for taekwondo performance. Soon, they get the address of the park with the date and time from Carl.

14

In preparation for her taekwondo performance, Bora makes a scheme to give the instruction on how to punch and kick with both arms and legs alternately and how to punch the air repeatedly for one minute straight. Since she has been well disciplined from the age of 8 without missing a single taekwondo class, she is used to some basic skills of self-defense enough to know how to teach punching and kicking techniques. As a black belt, she has won many medals in Korean taekwondo contests and her taekwondo skill is superior to that of experts, even though her agile action against some danger has been known to only Wan and Lang. On the first day of her arrival in LA, Bora was asked to teach taekwondo techniques by her twin cousins, but she couldn't keep doing it due to their hectic schedule. Therefore, her suggestion to teach Kate taekwondo in front of her friends may be natural for Bora to make this a memorable event, let alone her intention to intimidate Kate. Bora promises herself that she'll do her best.

On the day when the meeting is held, Bora and Lang look up at the sky in the kitchen while packing two boxes of cupcake and an icebox with beverages.

"Bora, the weather is nice for a picnic. I don't think there are people in the park because it's surrounded by houses."

"Yeah? It's almost nine o'clock. Let's go."

They arrive at the park first thing. Like Lang said, Bora sees no one around the park in which there are some cooling shades formed by several big trees. Bora puts a portable table in the shade and Lang loads the table with cupcake boxes and an icebox.

"It looks nice. Oh, here come Jin and Brian. Hi!" Bora says loudly.

Brian gives Bora a big smile.

"Hi, Bora. Hi, Lang, it's good to see you again. I was wondering how you both hang out?" Brian says.

"We're having a good time, and you?" Bora says.

"Great. You know, thanks to Jin, my math's getting better."

While Brian has a talk with Bora, Jin stands close to Lang and says, "Lang, Bora cares so much about you. When you drove to the mall to help Carl, she called me to find out what was going on. You two are like real sisters, not half sisters, huh."

"Oh, really? I didn't know that she tried to get help from you. Anyway, I thank you for your attention to Bora. Were you born here?"

"Yep, I'm Korean American. I live with my dad and grandma, and my mom passed away. You know, I have a cousin who goes to SNU. Someday, I'll visit Korea to see her. I've never been there, so I'll be very excited by the visit."

At that time Carl and Henry walk toward them with a box of beer following Kate and Christine.

"Hey, how are you doing? These beers are for three of us, you know." Carl lifts the box.

"Yeah, yeah, I know," Kate says with a smile.

"It's nice for us to hang out, quiet and spacious." Christine looks around the park.

Guys, do you wanna watch me teach Kate Korean martial arts, taekwondo now?" Bora says.

"Yes!"

Bora shows several basic skills with kicks, and Brian especially looks exhilarated clapping real hard. Kate standing in front of Bora seems to be infatuated a bit with Bora's brisk action and powerful kick.

"Oh, Bora, you're awesome!" Kate shouts with surprise at Bora's strength.

"Thanks. You can do it too."

Then, Bora begins to show Kate how to kick and how to punch. A few minutes later, Kate's friends except Lang join Kate lining up in two rows to learn taekwondo motions. They all follow Bora's instruction with the shouts of concentration. They look serious while following each motion and it seems like that they are enjoying taekwondo. Bora shows an action and then walks around to correct their postures one by one. They are absorbed in basic skills with curiosity. Some neighbors who are on their morning walk with their dogs stop to watch them interestingly, but soon have gone away.

15

Lang glances at her watch wondering when Bora is going to stop teaching taekwondo for self-defense. She is about to feel bored while sitting on a park bench under the shade, but stays calm being patient because she knows that Bora will proceed with the training until her planned mission is accomplished.

At last the practice ends, in a second, Brian runs toward Lang wiping the sweat.

"It was fun." Brian takes out a bottle of water from the icebox and drinks it up.

Then, the rest of them gather around the table to have some drink.

"Thank you so much for the lesson, Bora. I'm gonna find a place I can take taekwondo class. I think this is for me. How about you, guys?" Jin says.

"I'll think about it. Oh, we're all in a sweat. Let's go swimming in the ocean."

"Sounds good, Carl. I'll pack up these things. It was boring to sit here watching." Lang stands up to clean up the table.

Lang looks at Bora to do together, but she finds that Bora isn't paying attention to anybody staring at somewhere over the trees behind her. Even though Lang doesn't look around to know what it is, she can see that Bora's shoulders seem to grow tense. Lang says to Bora that she'd better have some drink before they leave for the beach.

"Lang, shh! There are some guys behind trees." Bora makes a sign with her index finger.

At that moment Jin notices Bora who seems to be ready to do action against some attackers, and then she sees a human shadow between the trees behind Lang. She takes a few steps toward Bora.

"What's up? I can see it like you do."

"You do? I hope nothing will happen to us. But I'm ready."

In a minute, two thin men in hoods show up and approach them with hands in their pockets. They wear sunglasses and masks so as not to be recognized.

"Oh my! Who are they?" Jin says.

"Jin, stay still! No one except us has seen them coming," Bora says calmly.

Only after Christine and Kate turn around to go to the car after picking up their stuff from the table, they find that they have unwelcome guests.

"Oh, Henry, look at them," Kate whispers leaning her back against his shoulder.

"Well, they just walk across the park."

"I don't think so."

A minute later, one man in a hood says, "Hey, it's a nice sunny day. Can we join you?"

"No, we're leaving," Carl says as the oldest of the eight.

Only then does Carl realize what is going on worrying about safety of his friends.

"Too bad, then . . . leave your cell phones. We need them," the man says, keeping his distance.

"Yeah, you leave your cell phones and beat it," the other man says, pulling something from his pocket.

Everybody including Bora stands paralyzed when they see these men in hoods have weapons. One man points his handgun at them and the other one raises his pocket knife.

"Everybody freeze, please! Just put down your phone on the table one by one! We won't hurt you. We just want phones" the man with a gun says, moving his gun side to side.

Kate turns around and places her cell phone on the table first. And the rest of them obediently do the same without looking at the men. Each one seems to go through all the trouble by giving up his cell phone, and Lang gazes at Bora expecting her to do something right. Bora looks back at Lang when her turn comes, and she stands like a post.

"Hey, you with a square chin, you're the only one who didn't put down yours. Do it now! And go and stand next to your friends!" A man shouts to Bora.

"Alright, but mine is over there." Bora points to the bench.

The man with his handgun turns his head a bit to see where it is, and just then Bora kicks his hand hard with her left foreleg so that the gun falls from his hand and punches his face at the same time. And instantly she knocks the other man with a pocket knife down by doing a powerful turning kick while he is dumbfounded at her knockout blow to his companion. Two men in hoods end up on the ground in a flash, and they don't move as if they are faint.

Everybody on the scene is at a standstill, looking puzzled. A few seconds later Brian pushes the gun away from the man when he hears his name called. Carl and Henry follow Brian to grab two men in hoods who are still lying on the ground.

16

Bora picks up the handgun from the ground with her handkerchief to hand it over to Carl. Carl takes a serious look at it and says, "I think this is a toy gun."

"What? You're kidding. Let me see it," Henry says.

"Yeah, hmm . . . you're right. Let's raise them up anyway."

Henry and Brian raise two boys up one by one since each one is lying on the ground like the dead. When they are put on the bench, they open their eyes and look at each other staying tight-lipped finding they are kept under control. Carl approaches them with a toy gun in his hand while the others stand around the bench.

"Hey, did you threaten us with this toy, huh?" Carl snorts.

"It's ridiculous. Is this knife a toy? Uh-oh, it's real."

"Well, what on earth are you doing? Now, I can see that

you look a lot younger than us."

"Hey, kids, don't take off your sunglasses because no one here wanna know who you are."

"And, we won't call the cop 'cause we are unhurt."

"But, we wanna hear what brought you here? Did you plan to take away our phones from us?"

One boy looks up at Carl and shakes his head.

"No. We were just going past you, and we came up with an idea for money."

"And we could see the situation. You all were absorbed in practicing something, so we knew we wouldn't draw your attentions."

"We always carry these things, you know," the other boy says.

"How come?" Christine asks.

"For self-defense."

"Huh, don't you know these are sort of weapons?" Christine says with wide eyes.

"Okay, well, well . . . do you do drugs? So you need money, huh?" Jin asks.

"No, we don't. We just wanna have the new iPhone, but you know . . ."

"Are you two related?" Kate asks.

"Yes. We're cousins. Anyway, we're terribly sorry for this fuss."

"By the way, who's that woman? How could she knock us out in a second? Oh my gosh, it happened real quick. Gee, amazing!"

"You know what? You were lucky. I could kick you harder to death," Bora says, staring at the boys.

While looking at them who are avoiding Bora's gaze, Bora suggests that they'd better take martial art classes like taekwondo.

"Yeah, I think that's a good idea," Jin agrees with Bora.

A minute later, two boys beg Carl for mercy looking around, and glance at Bora who is standing next to them wondering if she will beat them down to turn them over to the police.

"Can we go? We promise it'll never happen again."

"Alright, you're free to go now. We believe you. Be good boys to your parents, please!" Carl says as the oldest one among them.

After watching two boys walk away, Carl claps his hands and says, "Let's move to the beach."

"Oh, we forgot to say this," Carl says.

"Thank you so much, Bora. We appreciate everything. Without you, we could have been in big trouble. We owe you one."

"Thank you, Bora!" They all clap together.

Lang and Bora head home to pick up a few things such as beach towels while the others drop by a fast-food restaurant to buy some burgers for lunch.

On the way to the beach where Carl and the others are waiting Lang and Bora get stuck in the heavy traffic.

"Oh, we're gonna get there 20 minutes behind. It can't be helped anyway."

"Lang, you know what? When I saw the two boys walk away, a boy crossed my mind. They reminded me of the incident that happened on the path of the Sungbok Stream this January."

"You mean the boy who was about to steal a box of a bracelet from Wan? I heard about it. Since then whenever I saw your bracelet, I thought of the boy who was knocked by you before he fled with it."

"Yeah, the boy was given some money by Wan because he needed food to fill him up. But those two boys aren't starving."

"Right, how dare they attempt to rob us with a fake gun to make money for a new iPhone. Besides, we outnumbered two boys, huh."

"But our cell phones would've been taken without your kicks. Bora, you did a good job. Thanks." Lang smiles at Bora.

"No problem."

"Oh, now the traffic is moving. We're gonna arrive soon."

Bora gets a message from Kate that says "where are you now?"

Bora writes back, "Lang pulls the car into the parking lot. We'll be with you shortly."

Bora and Lang look around to find where their friends nestle down in the crowded beach.

"Look, Bora, they are over there. Oh, it's far." Lang points to somewhere.

"Hi!" Bora raises her hand.

"Place your towels around here and sit. Let's eat. I'm starving," Henry says.

Carl and Henry sit on the sand with their swimming pants on.

"Oh, you guys already surfed?" Lang asks to Carl and

Henry.

"Yes. That's what we can do best," Carl says.

"Bora, you do martial arts, and we do surfing."

"Hey, guys, after eating, you can try if you want," Henry says.

"I've never surfed before, but I brought my swimsuit. Lang did it, too," Bora says, biting a large chunk of hamburger.

"Good for you," Kate says smiling at Bora.

Bora feels that Kate is gentle with her after the taekwondo practice. But Bora doesn't take it as it is, thinking that Kate is a mysterious and untrustworthy girl.

17

About a week passes before Bora gets a phone call from Jin. Jin says that she wants to have a farewell party for Bora who will go back to Korea a week later. Since Bora has no reason to reject her offer, she is willing to reply to the invitation to Jin's home party.

"Jin, I really thank you for your caring. Who's coming?"

"You know, eight people like before."

"I see. You'd better text Lang about your address and the date of the party. And thank you again, Jin."

"Don't mention it. See you then, sis Bora," Jin says, cheerfully.

On the day of the party Lang and Bora walk to the front door of Jin's house, looking around the street to see if someone arrived before them. When they are about to ring the doorbell, the door opens and an old lady speaks to them with a smile on her face.

"Hi, I'm Hyun Lee, Jin's grandma. You're Bora, right? I heard you go to the same school as my other granddaughter goes. Oh, this is meant to be, huh."

"I guess so," Bora says.

Hyun looks so excited that she seems to forget to leave them alone talking about her son's family who live in Seoul, and Joon Kim interrupts her.

"Mother, we'd better go now. By the way, I'm Joon, Jin's dad. Just enjoy the party and the food I made for both of you."

"Okay, sure. Bora, how can I get in touch with you when I visit Korea?"

"Jin has my phone number. You're always welcome, Mrs. Kim."

"Oh, thank you. How sweet of you to say so," Hyun says with a big smile.

"Mom, it's time to leave. Bye girls."

"See you at night. And we thank you for delicious feast," Jin says to Joon and Hyun.

"Wait a minute. What's in it?" Hyun points to a box of cupcakes.

"Oh, the cupcakes I made. Do you wanna try some, Mrs. Kim?" Bora opens the box.

"Not now, sweetie. Save some for me, Jin."

"Bye, thank you both," Bora and Lang say together, bowing to them.

"Good bye, it was nice meeting you, Lang and Bora," Joon says and shuts the door behind him.

As soon as the door is shut, Jin takes Bora and Lang to the kitchen to show how the kitchen island is loaded with delicious dishes.

"It's amazing!" Bora and Lang say at the same time.

Soon, all eight people gather in the kitchen which flows into the living room after the recent remodeling. Henry walks around the living room and opens a French door to a screened porch. Then he steps on the decked veranda and says loudly to Jin.

"Here's an awning deck. We can sit around here."

"Come over to the table, Henry."

"Hey, guys, help yourself to some food. I bet you'll like it.

My dad is a good cook. He's a math teacher though."

"Yep, wow, great dishes!"

"I'll try Korean bibimbab and steamed galbi." Brian puts two foods on his plate.

"Gee, I'll have bulgogi and sweet chicken on a stick."

All of them sit around a table in the living room because of heat outside. They are quiet for a while enjoying dishes.

"Each dish is surprising and delightful. I really like all dishes," Christine says.

"Yeah, your dad is a good cook." Kate winks at Jin.

"I've tasted this real Korean food in a month," Bora says, smiling.

"I feel great today. You know, it was a shame that I grumbled at my dad who made a noise while cooking every Saturday morning. His cooking is worth it in the end."

"Jin, I'll do the dishes. Jin, you can show these guys around your home." Bora rises to her feet.

Brian follows Bora and begins to give a hand with the mess on the table.

"Oh, Bora, please don't. Christine and I'll do. You and Lang are guests."

The kitchen island is cleaned by Brian while Christine and

Kate put plates in the dishwasher.

When Carl and three others come to the living room with Jin after looking around the house, Kate brings them together and says that she got something to confess in front of them. Everybody looks at Kate wondering what confession is like. Kate takes a deep breath before speaking.

"This isn't easy to say, but I want to be honest with you, guys. Frankly speaking, I was bad to Lang . . ." Kate drops her eyes.

At that point, Bora picks up on what Kate is going to say thinking that her instinct was right. She glances at Lang who is staring at Kate's lips.

"Lang, I'm so sorry for two things I've done to you. Nothing happened though."

"Kate, make it snappy. We're dying to know." Henry pushes Kate.

"Okay. I had a private tutor for math about four years ago. Her name is Jung, Lang and Bora's older cousin. Since I was a bit lazy at that time, I got scolded a few times by her. You know it wasn't that bad, but I felt indignant welling up in me and quit the math lesson two months later. I haven't seen her for years until I bumped into her last month, and saw Bora and Lang there. And then I came across Bora and Lang at a game room, you know." Kate takes a sip of coffee to moisten her lips.

Everybody in the room keeps silence.

"That night after I got their phone numbers, I had my mind made up to pay her back. I decided on a little revenge." Kate pauses and gulps.

"I guess what two things you did," Henry says, glancing at Lang.

"Kate, you don't have to say what you did to me. I understand you," Lang says, looking into Kate's eyes.

"Oh, Lang . . . I don't know what to say. But I have to say this. When we had pizza party, I had it all planned. I asked my brother to scare you beforehand. And I don't know the details of how he took you and Carl 'cause he didn't tell me about that. Lang, I'm terribly sorry. I don't excuse myself from two situations I made to screw you over." Kate drops her eyes.

"Kate, I'm okay as long as you feel regret. I'd like to apologize instead. Maybe Jung wouldn't have thought that she hurt you at that time. Let's not dwell on the past."

"Oh, Lang, you have a huge heart. Thank you so much

for your generosity. I'm touched and I'm ashamed. I was afraid of how you'd react if I tell the truth." Kate holds Lang's hands.

"To sum up, Kate did something wrong to Lang. But Lang doesn't mind it as her friend. Am I right?" Jin says with a big smile.

"Bora, I'd like to know what you're thinking," Kate says.

"To be frank with you, I suspected you when Lang and Carl were out of sight at the pizza party. And I had a nightmare that night and you were in that nightmare. Since then I've thought of you asking myself, what's her motive?"

"Really? I guess you have a hunch. So . . . will you forgive me? You know, I wanna be your friend." Kate smiles at Bora.

"Now, yes. You showed us great courage. Thank you, Kate."

After Bora saying, Jin and the others begin to clap.

"you guys are wonderful!"

"Now what? Let's go surfing!" Carl shouts and rises to his feet.

18

Bora looks around the room after packing her bag in which there are a few things with some souvenirs for her mother. She fixes her gaze at the window seat where she has looked at the ocean every morning while staying in the beach house in California. It seems that she doesn't want to leave the room. She lifts her bag with a sigh and goes downstairs. She sees her twin cousins at the bottom of the staircase, who are standing there to say farewell to Bora instead of going to the airport with Jung and Lang. After having a short talk with the twins, Bora steps out to the driveway to get in the car in which Jung and Lang are waiting for Bora.

"Let's hit the road. I'll miss this place," Bora says.

"Come on, Bora, we'll see you again in five months," Jung says.

"Absolutely, you can come over here whenever you want," Lang says.

They arrive at the airport a lot earlier than expected, and find that Bora has plenty of time before boarding since she has only a carry-on bag. Jung takes Bora and Lang to a cafe to kill time.

They are seated at a table, and Lang is dismayed when her cell phone goes off. She grabs her cell phone quickly.

"Oh, I forgot to put it on vibrate. It's Jin."

"Hi, Jin, what's up? What? Are you here with Kate and Christine? What a surprise! Come over to us." Lang's eyes widen in surprise.

A few minutes later three girls join Bora at the table.

"Surprised, huh? I have a good memory, you know. At my home you told me when you would leave LA, so I made a note of it, sis Bora."

"Yeah, I guess so . . . anyway I thank you all for coming. I'm touched. I didn't know I meant this much to you," Bora says.

"We love you, Bora."

"Hi, Jung, how have you been? You know, I was twisted. But there is nothing on my mind," Kate says.

"Kate, what's it all about?" Jung asks with a puzzled look.

"I mean I like you, Lang and Bora." Kate smiles at Jung.

"By the way, Bora, I think I'll miss you. You know what? I and Christine are gonna register the taekwondo class next week that Jin is in."

"Really? Great, I'm glad to hear that. Good for you," Bora says.

After a long talk, Bora stands up to get ready to board her flight.

"I have to go. Girls, and sis Jung, thank you so much for your time. See you next time."

"Alright, Bora, have a good flight. Say hello to your mother." Jung hugs Bora.

Then, Lang and the other three girls hug Bora.

"Bye for now! Oh, I forgot to tell you this, I saw the two boys in the taekwondo class. I mean two young robbers. They told me to say thank you to you. You know what? You did a great job." Jin says with a big smile.

"Oh, really? It went well."

"Jin! Kate! Christine! I wanna say a word about my first visit to LA. In a word, I'm lucky that I got to know you." Bora makes a heart with fingers.

Sisters
A Summer Vacation

초판 1쇄 발행일 | 2021년 12월 15일

지은이 | 김학진
펴낸이 | 김동명
펴낸곳 | 도서출판 창조와 지식
디자인 | 주식회사 북모아
인쇄처 | 주식회사 북모아

출판등록번호 | 제2018-000027호
주소 | 서울특별시 강북구 덕릉로 144
전화 | 1644-1814
팩스 | 02-2275-8577

ISBN 979-11-6003-409-7

값 10,000원

이 책은 저작권법에 따라 보호받는 저작물이므로 무단 전재와 무단 복제를 금지하며,
이 책 내용을 이용하려면 반드시 저작권자와 도서출판 창조와 지식의 서면동의를 받아야 합니다.
잘못된 책은 구입처나 본사에서 바꾸어 드립니다.

지식의 가치를 창조하는 도서출판 창조와 지식
www.mybookmake.com